GHOST DETECTORS
Doggone!

BOOK 20

BY
ADRIENNE ENDERLE

ILLUSTRATED BY
DAVE SHEPHARD

Calico

An Imprint of Magic Wagon
abdopublishing.com

Contents

Chapter 1
Haunted Bakery

Malcolm's mouth watered as he gazed down at the brownie on his plate. No one made brownies better than Flour Power Bakery. Not only were they delicious, they were as thick as a ham sandwich and as big as a math book. And that was before the whipped cream and sprinkles!

"See how much you can cram in your mouth at once," Malcolm's best friend, Dandy, dared him.

Malcolm took a giant lick of the whipped cream, cold and smooth on his tongue. Then he picked up the brownie, opened wide, and chomped. *Yummmmm . . .* He didn't even care that some got plastered across his chin and cheeks.

"What are you waiting for?" he asked Dandy.

Dandy looked down at his own colossal cupcake with its Incredible Hulk–green frosting. He ran a finger across the top, scooping up a massive glob of the sugary, buttery frosting. Just before it reached his mouth, Dandy's finger twitched, flicking the frosting—*splat!*—onto Malcolm's nose.

Malcolm crossed his eyes and looked down at the green glob. "Hey! What gives?"

"I didn't do it on purpose," Dandy answered. "My finger jerked." Before

Malcolm could wipe it off, Dandy reached over and scraped it back onto his finger. "I'm not wasting this."

He brought it to his mouth again. *Whack!* It flew off, hitting Malcolm's ear.

"Will you stop it?" Malcolm yelled.

"I'm sorry," Dandy said. "My finger is jerky today." He scooped off the frosting and brought it quickly to his mouth. But just as it got close, his finger flicked again.

The frosting took flight, sailing past Malcolm and hitting the backside of a woman who was bending over to pick up her purse. She popped up and looked around to see where it had come from.

"Oops," Dandy said under his breath. He examined his finger, bending it like he was calling someone over. "That's so weird. I'm really not trying to do anything."

Malcolm looked up as a group of Flour Power waiters marched out of the kitchen carrying an enormous pink cake with five lit candles. They smiled proudly in their lime-green chef's coats and muffin-shaped chef's hats.

The crew set the cake in the middle of a long table of kindergartners and a few adults as they sang "Happy Birthday." Everyone at the table joined in with, "Happy birthday, dear Daisy!"

Once the song was sung, little Daisy closed her eyes, making her wish. Then she sucked in a breath, opened her eyes, and—

All the candles went out on their own.

Huh? "Did you see that?" Malcolm asked Dandy. Dandy nodded.

Daisy looked at the cake in surprise, and then looked up at her parents.

"It's okay, sweetie," said a lady who must have been her mom. "We'll relight them."

One of the waiters pointed to the ceiling. "Sorry. That air conditioner vent is really strong." The staff moved fast to light the candles again. They sang the song all over. Daisy took a deep breath and—

The candles went out by themselves.

Daisy's lip began to quiver as she held back tears.

The Flour Power crew scrambled to relight the candles a second time. Everyone hovered so no wind could blow out the candles before Daisy could do it herself.

"Make a wish," her mom said, hurriedly.

Daisy closed her eyes, sucked in a deep breath, and blew. The candles went out, but the gust was so strong it picked up the entire cake and shot it across the table. It slapped down on top of a thin, bald man in a golf shirt.

"Oh, Uncle Herman, I'm so sorry," Daisy's mom said.

Daisy couldn't hold it back any longer. "Waaaaahhhhh!"

Dandy scrunched down, covering his ears. "Wow! She's half our age, but she sounds like a police siren."

"Only louder," Malcolm added.

"Nobody can blow that hard," Dandy said.

Malcolm nodded.

"My caaaaaaake!" Daisy wailed.

While two of the waiters plucked the cake off Uncle Herman's head, a waitress said to Daisy, "Don't worry, we'll get you another cake."

"You bet you will!" Daisy's mom yelled like it was the bakery's fault. The waitress ran off to check on the replacement cake.

Malcolm pushed aside his brownie and leaned toward Dandy. "Seriously, that kid probably couldn't blow a napkin off a straw. How'd she do that?"

Dandy shrugged. "I don't know."

Just as the waiters were picking the last of the cake crumbs off Uncle Herman's head, all the party plates rose into the air.

Daisy's mom stomped her foot. "What in the world is—" But before she could finish, the plates spun across the room like Frisbees.

That's when Malcolm overheard one waiter say to another, "I told you this place is haunted."

Yep, Malcolm thought. *Definitely.*

Chapter 2
Where's Spooky?

Malcolm and Dandy quickly biked back to Malcolm's house.

"All right," Malcolm said as they stepped onto the porch. "We get in, grab the gear, and get back to the bakery." He could only imagine what disaster could be happening. A tart tornado? A sticky bun blizzard? He opened the front door and—

"Ahh!" he yelled, stumbling back into Dandy. Malcolm's sister, Cocoa, stood at the threshold, her orange-tinted hair

frizzing out in all directions. Her puke-green glossy lips curled into a snarl.

"Out of my way, twerp!" Cocoa growled, pushing past him. "I'm late."

Malcolm dodged to the side. "For what?"

Cocoa gave him a death glare. Her yellow striped skirt billowed out like a tutu. "I've got a date with destiny."

"Who's Destiny?" Dandy asked.

She rolled her eyes. "I'm on my way to a modeling audition at the mall."

Her? A model? Malcolm wiggled a finger in his ear, certain he had not heard right.

Cocoa tugged Malcolm's finger from his ear. "You're so gross!" Then she twirled on her purple platform heels and marched away.

"Make sure to stop by Flour Power!" Malcolm yelled to her.

Dandy grinned.

"I'd love to see her plastered in pink frosting," Malcolm said under his breath.

They hurried to the basement to collect their ghost-fighting equipment. After all, Malcolm and Dandy had a reputation to fulfill as the Ghost Detectors. With their specter detector and ghost zapper, they could stop any haunting, anywhere.

"Do you think they'll pick Cocoa to model?" Dandy asked as he shook the ghost zapper to see if it had enough juice.

"Yeah. If they're looking for the Clown Bride of Frankenstein." Malcolm tossed Dandy a bag of potato chips. "Fuel up."

Dandy ripped open the bag, a salty aroma wafting out. "Thanks." His mouth dropped into a frown. "I didn't get to eat any of my cupcake."

"Don't worry," Malcolm told him. "Once we get rid of the Flour Power ghost, they'll probably reward you with a year's supply."

Dandy grinned.

Malcolm powered up the specter detector to make sure it was fully charged. But something was off. He could feel it. He stood still, listening.

Dandy chomped on some potato chips.

Malcolm put his finger to his lips. "Shh."

Dandy froze, a chip hanging from his mouth, potato flakes on his chin. "I don't hear anything," he whispered, chips garbling his words.

"That's the problem," Malcolm said. "Where's Spooky?"

Malcolm turned in a circle, looking for his little phantom dog. Spooky always showed up when the detector was on, greeting

Malcolm with a *Yip! Yip!* But the dog was nowhere to be seen. That just didn't make sense.

Dandy shrugged, licking potato chip dust off his fingers. "Maybe he just went outside for a walk or something."

Malcolm tilted his head. "Alone?"

Dandy started to look a little panicky.

"Let's go," Malcolm said, grabbing their gear. "The bakery ghost can wait. We've got to find Spooky first."

Dandy followed, rolling the top of the potato chip bag to a close. "I hope he hasn't gone very far."

"Me too," Malcolm said, but he had a sinking feeling in his gut.

Chapter 3
Dognapped!

Malcolm biked down the street, the ghost detector charged and bleeping.

"How are we going to find him?" Dandy asked.

Malcolm had no clue, but one thing was for sure—he'd do whatever it took to get Spooky back. "Let's just keep riding up and down the blocks. He can't have gotten too far, right?"

They made a left at the next street.

Why would Spooky leave? Malcolm wondered. *Where would he go?*

Dandy, eyes on his surroundings, nearly slammed into a parked car. He quickly dodged it and kept his balance. Malcolm could see the worry on Dandy's face.

"What if we don't find him?" Dandy asked.

"We will," Malcolm said, swerving around some trash cans. "We have to."

"Maybe we should put up missing posters," Dandy suggested. "And offer a reward. I could pitch in some money."

"You're forgetting," Malcolm said, "he's a ghost."

Dandy slumped a bit. "He's just so real."

Malcolm knew exactly how Dandy felt. Spooky was more than just his pet. That faithful pooch had even saved his life once.

He had to find him. They pedaled in silence, keeping their eyes peeled.

The specter detector kept searching too. *Bleep. Bleep-bleep.* But soon—*bleep-bleep-bleep-bleep-bleep-bleep-bleep-bleep-bleep-bleep-bleep*—the thing went haywire!

Please be him! Malcolm pleaded silently.

"There!" Dandy yelled, pointing to his right, swerving as he let go of the handlebar.

Malcolm looked to where Dandy pointed. Spooky was bounding down the sidewalk, his tongue lolling. *Yip! Yip! Yip!*

Malcolm hopped off his bike, abandoning it on the curb. "Spooky!" he called, racing after him.

But the dog wasn't listening. He scampered at record speed, his paws flying.

Dandy caught up to Malcolm, matching his stride. "What's he chasing?"

Malcolm narrowed his eyes. He'd been so focused on catching Spooky, he hadn't realized why the dog was on the move. Something slithered in front of Spooky, just out of his reach. *A snake? Wait . . . no.* Then Malcolm realized what was making Spooky so spunky. "He's chasing a string of sausages!"

Dandy's eyes bulged. "Huh?"

Malcolm had seen lots of weird things before, but this was impossible. Sausages don't come to life and fly down a sidewalk. There was definitely something going on.

The boys continued after Spooky, huffing and puffing. The string of sausages kept its pace, bouncing ahead. Every time Spooky thought he had it, the sausage links would pick up speed.

"How's it doing that?" Dandy asked.

Malcolm wished he knew. He kept his eyes on it, trying to figure it out.

"There!" Malcolm called, pointing. Just ahead, he saw something tall and skinny sticking out of a bush. *A fishing pole?* His heart raced as fast as the sausages when he realized what was going on. "It's a trap!"

He powered his arms, running with all his might. "Spooky! No! Stop!"

The sausage string came to a halt just under the bush. And so did Spooky, skidding on his paws.

"Spooky!" Malcolm and Dandy yelled.

But it was too late. A large butterfly net swung down, right on top of Spooky.

"Gotcha!" a young man yelled, jumping out of the bushes. He was built like a bean pole with a face full of zits. His dogcatcher uniform bagged around him, and he wore a

dirty baseball cap cocked toward the back of his head. Malcolm saw a name sewn above the guy's pocket: Bud. Bud swooped up the net and bounded off, the string of sausages trailing behind him.

"Hey! That's my dog!" Malcolm yelled.

The dogcatcher hurried around the corner, never looking back. Malcolm pumped his legs harder, racing to catch up. He rounded the curb just in time to see a large brown van zoom off. A sign on the side read:

Chapter 4
Hatching a Plan

Dandy ran up next to Malcolm, panting. He hunched over, hands on his knees, trying to catch his breath. "Where'd . . . the . . . guy . . . go?"

Malcolm stared down the street. "He's gone."

"What do you mean he's gone?"

"He snatched Spooky and drove off." Malcolm angrily kicked his foot against the curb, thinking it would make him feel better. But it made his big toe ache instead.

Dandy looked at Malcolm, his eyebrows knit together. "So what now? We go after him, right?"

Malcolm was still too upset to think.

"Right?" Dandy waved his hand in front of Malcolm's face. "That dude looked like a ghost. And that's what we do, remember? We go after ghosts. We can stop this guy and get Spooky back."

Malcolm snapped out of his anger and looked at Dandy. "Wow, when did you become so fearless?"

Dandy blew out a long breath. "The second that guy stole our dog."

The boys headed back to Malcolm's basement, fired up and ready to research. Sure, someone at Flour Power Bakery could

be getting chocolate chips crammed up his nose, but that haunting had to wait. There were bigger problems at hand.

Dandy picked up Spooky's rubber ball and bounced it against the wall. "So what does Apparition Animal Control mean?"

Malcolm opened his laptop. "An apparition is a ghost. And animal control picks up stray critters."

Dandy threw the ball too hard. It boomeranged back and bonked him on the head. "But that guy didn't pick up Spooky. He baited him."

"I know," Malcolm said. "The creep."

Dandy bounced the ball again. This time it shot off the wall and knocked over an empty soda can. "But that's cheating."

"I know," Malcolm said. "And why snatch animal ghosts?"

Dandy retrieved the ball. "Those poor things. What did they ever do? They're just innocent little ghosts. So what if they leave ectoplasm on the carpet once in a while."

He pitched the ball hard. It ricocheted off the wall, bouncing up to the ceiling and back down to the floor before shooting up again and whacking him in the chin. "Ow." He set the ball aside and stood next to Malcolm.

Just the thought of those caged animals made Malcolm's blood boil. But if he wanted to get Spooky back, he'd have to remain calm.

Dandy gazed over Malcolm's shoulder as he searched online. He typed in *Apparition Animal Control*. Nothing came up. He tried *ghost dog pound*. No luck. Malcolm continued to search, but he ended up with a big fat pile of nothing. He shut his laptop and drooped.

"Are we giving up?" Dandy asked.

Malcolm shook his head. "No way."

"But we don't know where to look."

Malcolm tapped his finger on his computer, thinking. "Where would we find other ghost dogs?"

"What?" Panic washed over Dandy's face. "You want to replace Spooky already?"

"No," Malcolm said, "but if we knew where there were other dogs like Spooky, maybe we could set a trap of our own."

Dandy scratched his nose. "You mean bring our own net and sausage links?"

A plan began to form in Malcolm's head. "No, just our specter detector and ghost zapper. The guy won't stand a chance."

"Okay," Dandy said, "but where do we find other ghost dogs?"

Malcolm thought about the day Spooky followed him home. He and Dandy had just

zapped a nasty spirit at a house where he'd been dogsitting. He hadn't realized Spooky was a ghost. But Malcolm didn't care. He loved Spooky so much.

Malcolm opened his laptop and typed the words *dog ghosts*. Several links popped up, all with the same two words: *pet cemetery*.

Chapter 5
Always & Furever

"**P**erfect," Malcolm said, a smile stretching across his face. He did a web search for pet cemeteries nearby and found a write-up in a blog called *Strange Happenings*. Malcolm read:

Always & Furever Pet Cemetery - The Most Haunted Place in Town

Think your pet is a little angel? Not if it's buried at Always & Furever. Strange happenings are going on there for sure! Pet owners claim when they visit

the cemetery, they can hear their beloved companions calling to them.

Rita Redly reported that her Chihuahua, Reynolds, yaps at her every time she takes flowers to his grave. Dan Smith claims his parrot, Ivan, squawks "Peekaboo!" when he visits. And Mary Folger feels her cat, Penelope, rub against her legs each time she's there.

We at Strange Happenings investigated. It's true. Our recordings picked up all manner of animal sounds.

Malcolm played the recordings. Sure, they could've been from the woods next to the cemetery. But he refused to believe it. If people haunted human cemeteries, then he figured animals haunted pet cemeteries.

"Let's go," he said to Dandy, closing his laptop.

Dandy hopped up. "Do you think this will work?"

Malcolm shrugged. "Right now, it's all we've got. And who knows, maybe Ivan the parrot can say more than 'peekaboo' and fill us in on some things."

He snatched up his pack of equipment, and the boys headed up the basement stairs. Just as they opened the door—

"WAHOO!"

Dandy froze, a look of horror on his face. "What was that?"

"Uh . . . I don't know," Malcolm said. "It sounds like an ape is loose in the house."

They crept down the hallway and peeked around the corner. Cocoa was in the middle of the living room, jumping and dancing.

"Oh yeah," Malcolm said to Dandy. "An ape *is* loose in the house."

"A-huh, a-huh, a-huh-a-huh-a-huh," Cocoa sang.

Dandy watched, blank-faced. "Your sister's really happy about something."

Malcolm rolled his eyes. "Maybe there was a two-for-one sale on Glitter Gunk makeup."

Cocoa continued her happy dance, leaping and pirouetting. But when she kicked, her purple high heel flew off her foot and hit Dandy between the eyes.

"Ow!" Dandy placed a hand to his injury.

"Hey!" she yelled, limping toward them on one bare foot. "I need my shoe back."

Malcolm tried not to stare at her toenails, but each one was painted silver with a violet eyeball peeking up. It was like a five-eyed monster stomping toward them. "Take your old shoe," Malcolm said,

kicking it toward her. "What are you so happy about anyway?"

She picked up her shoe and then stuck her nose in the air. "Wouldn't *you* like to know?"

Actually, he would. *Did Mom or Dad up her allowance?* Malcolm wondered.

"But I'm not going to tell you," she continued, pretending to be regal. "We models don't have time for regular people."

Malcolm blinked a few times, not believing his ears. "They actually want you to model?"

"Of course," Cocoa said. "Just *look* at me." She struck a pose, one hand on her hip, the other on her head.

Malcolm snickered. "I didn't know they hired models at the Halloween store. The gorilla costume will look great on you."

Cocoa kicked her other shoe at Malcolm, missing him and hitting Dandy again.

"Ow! Will you stop that?" Dandy whined.

"For your information," Cocoa said, her lip curled, "I'll be modeling for Fashion

Passion, the trendiest shop in the mall. They want me to be in their runway show tomorrow."

"Cocoa," Mom called from the kitchen, "don't forget, the show's for a good cause."

"I know, Mom!" Cocoa looked at Malcolm and smirked. "All the money from the fashion show goes to the soup kitchen downtown. But there will be tons of talent scouts there. You'll see. I'm going to be *famous*."

"Yeah," Malcolm mumbled. "Famous for falling on your face."

She reared, shoe in hand, and Dandy ducked.

"Malcolm," he squeaked, "maybe we should go."

"Yes, go!" Cocoa hollered. "I need to practice."

Dandy rubbed his head as he skirted around her. "Good luck."

Cocoa placed her hands on her hips and flipped back her hair. "Luck? Ha! I don't need luck."

"Right," Malcolm agreed. "You need a paper bag over your head."

They raced out just as her shoe hit the door.

"Let's hurry," Malcolm said, looking at the afternoon shadows stretching across the yard.

Dandy nodded, a bump forming between his eyes. "Yeah. I don't want to be stuck in that cemetery after dark, even if the ghosts are cute and cuddly."

Chapter 6
Ghostly Graveyard

The enormous gate that led into Always & Furever Pet Cemetery loomed high over Malcolm and Dandy as they chained their bikes to the iron fence.

"Wow," Malcolm said. "Most human cemeteries aren't this fancy."

Dandy chewed his lower lip. "Looks creepy to me."

Malcolm couldn't argue with that. Two pointy-eared dog statues stood on either side of the gate, looking more like fiendish

hounds than happy pets. He glanced up at a bird sculpture above them. He couldn't tell if it was a canary or a rabid bat.

"Let's go." Malcolm hoisted his pack onto his shoulder. He expected the gate to creak, but it swung wide open with one small push.

They stepped in quietly and glanced around. It looked like a little village, with gravestones shaped like doghouses, goldfish bowls, and birdcages. But Malcolm was more agog over the bushes scattered around. Each bush was shaped like an animal. He spotted a dachshund, a sphynx cat, a turtle, and . . . was that a rhinoceros?

"Uh . . . do you think there's a real rhino buried in here?" he asked Dandy.

"Maybe," Dandy answered, pointing to a shrub beyond it. "It could be buried next to the T. rex."

They turned and strolled down a path called Feathered Friends Lane. Malcolm wasn't sure why it was named that since most of the graves along it were dogs and cats. But a few weren't. He read a few headstones:

FUZZY
WE WILL NEVER SHED YOU
FROM OUR THOUGHTS
THE WAY YOU SHED ON OUR COUCH

OUR BELOVED HAMSTER REMY
MAY YOUR HEAVENLY HAMSTER
WHEEL ALWAYS BE OILED

SILVIA
THE BEST SNAKE EVER
YOU SLITHERED INTO OUR LIVES
AND COILED IN OUR HEARTS

Reading those sweet epitaphs made Malcolm miss Spooky terribly. He felt even more determined to find him. He unzipped his pack and took out the specter detector.

"Wait," Dandy said, his eyes wide. "What if some of these pets weren't tame? We could get stampeded, or bitten, or have our eyes pecked out!"

Malcolm looked at one of the graves:

GORDON GECKO
OUR LUCKY LIZARD

"I think we can take that chance," he said. He hit the power button, and the detector began its usual *bleep-bleep-bleep.*

So far, so good. No stampedes or attacks. They crept along the different paths as the sun sank lower in the sky.

"Something's wrong," Malcolm said, looking left and right.

"What?" Dandy asked, tiptoeing up next to him. He looked like he was expecting a snake to slither up his leg.

Malcolm stopped next to a giraffe-shaped bush. "We're in a cemetery with the specter detector on. The place should be overrun with animal spirits."

Dandy scratched his head. "Are you sure it's working?"

Malcolm examined the device. *Bleep. Bleep-bleep. Bleep-bleep.*

Just then, a gruff voice behind them called out, "It's working just fine."

Both boys jumped at the sound. Dandy started to topple, but Malcolm caught him before he fell splat onto the grave of Peanut the toy poodle.

Malcolm whipped around toward the voice. An old man leaned against a penguin-shaped shrub. His faded overalls and ratty straw hat were smeared with dirt, just like the work gloves hanging out of his pocket.

"Who are you?" Malcolm asked.

"Name's Digger," the man said. "I used to take care of this place before . . . well, you know."

Malcolm did know. The guy had ghost written all over him.

Chapter 7
Digger and Farrah

"**D**igger?" Dandy asked. "Like . . . gravedigger?" He gulped.

Digger nodded. "I prefer the term caretaker myself."

It wasn't until he took a step toward them that Malcolm realized the ghost hadn't been leaning on the penguin-shaped shrub after all. Digger's shoulders hunched so far he looked like a question mark. Malcolm figured the old guy must have dug graves all his life.

Digger hobbled closer to the boys. "Anyhoo, you're wasting your time. You won't find what you're looking for. Not here." He took off his hat and tried to brush away some of the dirt.

Malcolm cocked his head, wondering. "What is it you think we're looking for?" he asked.

Digger pointed a knotty finger at him. "Well, you've come to a pet cemetery with some sort of ghost-seeing contraption. Even a simple guy like me can piece it together. But, like I said, you won't find what you're looking for."

"Why not?" Malcolm asked. "Where are all the ghosts?"

"Missing," he said. "Some pimple-faced youngster came in with a net, scooped 'em up, and hauled 'em off."

"All of them?" Malcolm asked.

A grin crept across Digger's face and he winked. "All except Farrah."

Malcolm and Dandy shared a glance. Then Dandy asked, "Who's Farrah?"

Just as the words left Dandy's mouth, a small, furry head popped up from the bib of Digger's overalls.

Wait, Malcolm thought. *Is that a—*

"A ferret!" Dandy shouted.

Digger's grin widened. "There's my girl."

Farrah the ferret slinked down to the ground. She scampered toward Dandy, her nose wiggling as she sniffed the air.

Farrah ran circles around Dandy as he stood stone-still, his eyes as wide as dinner plates. Then, she hopped onto his sneaker, circled up his leg, and settled on his shoulder.

"M . . . Malcolm," Dandy whispered, his voice weak and shaky.

Digger laughed. "Don't you worry about her. She's as harmless as a newborn kitten."

Malcolm believed it, but he wasn't so sure about Dandy. Farrah and Dandy were nose to nose, neither of them making a move.

"Why wasn't she taken?" Malcolm asked Digger. "Didn't the animal control guy try to scoop her up, too?"

"Yep," Digger answered. "Several times."

Farrah cocked her head this way and that, like she was as confused about Dandy as he was about her.

"But," Digger continued, "he can't hold my little sweetheart there. She's too slippery for 'im. She always came bounding back."

"I wish he'd come get her now," Dandy whined, craning his head back.

Digger let out a piercing whistle. Farrah dashed back down to the ground and scurried to the old man. Dandy sighed in relief.

"Do you know where we can find him?" Malcolm asked Digger. "It's really important. He took our dog."

Digger's face dropped into a frown. "I'm sorry to hear that." He snapped his fingers

toward Farrah. She ran up and nestled into his overalls again. "I'm afraid I don't know where he's taking 'em all. But if I were you, I'd try the local animal shelter."

"Furs & Purrs Animal Shelter?" Malcolm asked. "With living, breathing strays?"

Digger nodded. "That'd be the one."

Malcolm had figured the pimply ghost had Spooky locked away somewhere, but he hadn't thought of the real animal shelter.

Digger looked at the sky. "The sun's setting. Y'all best get home. You wouldn't want to be riding home after dark. Believe me, not all ghosts are as friendly as me."

That was something Malcolm knew all too well.

"And another thing," Digger said. "Stay away from the mall bakery. I hear it's haunted."

Word about Flour Power was getting around. "Thank you," Malcolm said. He nudged Dandy, who still had his eyes on Farrah's denim nest.

Digger took off his dirt-caked hat and waved it before disappearing behind the penguin shrub.

Malcolm clicked off his specter detector and placed it in his pack. "He's right. We need to get home."

"Yeah," Dandy agreed, looking down at his shoulder. "Plus, Farrah left something on my shirt." He touched his finger to the green glob. "I hope our laundry detergent can get out ectoplasm."

Chapter 8
Furs & Purrs

By the time Malcolm got home, his stomach was rumbling loudly. And it was spaghetti night! He could practically smell the heaping pile of tomatoey pasta all the way from the pet cemetery.

But when he opened the front door, all he got a whiff of was Grandma Eunice, who always smelled like foot powder and skin ointment. She sat at the dining table with an old-timey boom box where his bowl of spaghetti should have been.

"Grandma? Where's dinner?"

"Shh . . ." She put a knotty finger to her lips. Then, with that same finger, she pressed a button on the boom box.

Malcolm covered his ears as a blast of techno music shot from the speakers. But as loud as the music was, it still couldn't drown out his sister.

"Move!" Cocoa screeched. Malcolm ducked behind Grandma Eunice's wheelchair.

Cocoa pranced into the room wearing a long red dress with black dots, white stockings, and dark green high heels. She looked like a slice of watermelon. Her arms were extended in a regal position and a textbook was balanced on her head.

"Come on, honey," Grandma Eunice cheered. "You've got it! You've got it!"

Malcolm doubled over in laughter. "You know that's not how you study, right?"

"Shut it, smarty!" Cocoa squawked. "This is important."

"There you go," Grandma Eunice called out. "Now, pose!"

Cocoa froze, the textbook wobbling like a boat in a storm.

"How is this more important than dinner?" Malcolm asked.

Cocoa glared at him. "I'm practicing for tomorrow." She turned, jutting her hip.

"That's right," Grandma said, clapping her hands. "Walk that catwalk, girlfriend!"

Malcolm rolled his eyes and sighed. It was hopeless. "But what's for dinner?"

Cocoa's face turned as red as her dress. "Oh, for goodness' sake! Can't you see this is more important?" She spun and wiggled the other way.

Whatever, Malcolm thought. He went to the pantry and pulled out the peanut butter.

Just as he opened the jar, Grandma Eunice hollered, "C'mon, girl. Shake what your great-grandma gave ya!"

Malcolm put the lid back on. Maybe he wasn't so hungry after all.

Malcolm woke up on Saturday morning raring to go. The animal shelter was just two blocks from the mall, so he and Dandy hitched a ride with Malcolm's family.

But all the way there, they had to listen to Malcolm's mom, dad, and great-grandma

blab about how beautiful Cocoa would be walking the runway and how nice it was that she was supporting the community.

Ugh.

"You're not staying to watch?" Malcolm's mom asked as they settled into chairs set up for the fashion show.

Malcolm slumped. "Mom, I don't need to know what all the middle school girls will be wearing this spring." Even if he didn't have to rescue Spooky, he'd just get in trouble for laughing at Cocoa.

His mom sighed. "Okay. But be back here in two hours."

Malcolm rounded his fingers in the OK sign and nudged Dandy. Then he slung his pack on his shoulder and they raced out the side exit. They ran all the way to the animal shelter.

The boys pushed through the glass doors and into a large room with checkered tile floors and an L-shaped desk. A young woman in a brown polo shirt and khaki pants beamed up from behind the desk. Her name tag read:

"Welcome to Furs & Purrs. What can I do for you?" Annie asked.

"My dog is missing," Malcolm said. "May we check to see if he's here?"

A pout formed on her lips. "Of course you can. Just go right through that door," she said, pointing.

Malcolm nodded. "Thanks."

Annie gave him a sympathetic smile. "I hope your doggie is here."

"Me too," Malcolm said.

The holding area looked like a giant tunnel lined with pens. The sounds of woofs and meows echoed throughout.

There were people milling around, pointing and oohing. Malcolm hoped some of the animals would get adopted that day.

He partially unzipped his pack and clicked on the specter detector without removing it.

Dandy's eyes popped wide. "Aren't you afraid people will see the ghosts?"

"I can't worry about that right now," Malcolm said. "This is our only chance."

They strolled down the long aisle, checking every pen. There were plenty of dogs, but they were all living and breathing.

Malcolm sighed as he drooped against a giant dog statue. "The dogcatcher didn't bring them here."

Dandy's mouth twitched. "So what do we do now?"

"I don't know." Malcolm felt like crying. This place was their only lead.

Dandy placed a hand on Malcolm's shoulder. "Don't worry. We'll find him."

But Malcolm wasn't so sure. He turned and adjusted his pack, ready to go.

That's when he noticed the plaque on the dog statue.

IN HONOR OF HARRIETT
OUR BRAVE FRIEND AND HERO HARRIETT
LOST HER LIFE ASSISTING FIREFIGHTERS IN
RESCUING THE ANIMALS FROM THE DEADLY FIRE
OF 1988. WE DEDICATE THIS STATUE AND THIS
FACILITY TO HER MEMORY.

"Did you see this?" Malcolm asked Dandy. "There was an animal shelter here before this one."

"Yeah," Dandy said. "Harriett must've been some great dog."

But Malcolm already had Dandy by the arm, tugging him through the door.

Annie looked up as they hurried back to the lobby. "Did you find your dog?"

"No," Malcolm replied, "but I read that there was another animal shelter that burned down. Do you know where it was located?"

Annie nodded eagerly. "Yes. They rebuilt part of it and tore down the rest. It's in the back. We use it for storage." She tilted her head. "But there are no animals living there."

Malcolm only smiled.

Chapter 9

Bud's Story

Malcolm and Dandy hurried to the storage building, looking around to make sure no one saw them. *Please be unlocked,* Malcolm thought, reaching for the door. It clicked open. *Yes!*

"I guess the shelter doesn't think anyone will steal puppy chow," he told Dandy.

With the ghost detector powered up, they crept around shelves of pet food, flea powder, and kitty litter.

Bleep-bleep.

Dandy tugged on Malcolm's shirt and pointed to a door in the back. Malcolm nodded and they edged toward it.

Bleep-bleep-bleep-bleep-bleep!

Jackpot! Malcolm swung open the door. Animal cages lined the room. Each one held the spirit of someone's long-lost pet.

Malcolm pointed his specter detector at the cages. "I'll check this side, and you check that side," he said to Dandy. "Spooky's here. I just know it."

He could barely look at the animals inside each pen. They all moped, with sagging ears and drooping tails. Even the snake, whom he guessed was Silvia, was coiled sadly in the corner of her cage.

"I don't get it," Dandy said, his back to Malcolm. "They're ghosts. They can pass through anything. What's holding them?"

"Good question," said Malcolm. That's when he heard: *Yip! Yip!*

"Spooky!"

They dashed toward the sound, Malcolm's heart beating wildly.

"Here he is!" Dandy said.

Yip! Yip! Spooky looked so small, his tail wagging. *Yip! Yip!*

"Don't worry, boy," Malcolm said. "I'll get you out." He reached for the cage door, but the second he touched it—*pop!*—a spark shot up his hand, sending a shock wave down his arm. "Ow!" He jumped back, shaking it limply.

"Well, now we know what's holding them in," Dandy said.

Malcolm looked at his burned fingers.

"The cages are electrified. We have to find out how to turn it off," Dandy said.

They searched the room up and down, careful not to get another zap.

"Is this it?" Dandy called, reaching for a large red switch.

"Don't touch it!" a ghostly voice ordered.

Malcolm turned just in time to see Bud, the dogcatcher, charging in. He was holding his net.

Swish! Bud scooped up Dandy in the net.

"Hey!" Dandy yelled. He kicked his feet against the web of ropes, tangling himself inside.

Malcolm dug out his ghost zapper and dashed toward them.

But Bud was quick. With a wave of his hand, the air whirled like a tornado. The noise of the wind drowned out the barking and meowing as pellets of kitty litter whipped about.

Malcolm pushed against the storm, his body fighting forward. He held up his arm, shielding his eyes from the flying kitty litter. "Why are you doing this?" he yelled.

Bud's lip curled. "Because," he answered, "I hate animals! They bite, they scratch, they smell. I devoted my life to getting them off the streets! But then one day a mangy mutt bit me, and I didn't live to tell the tale."

He's telling the tale now, Malcolm thought.

"But these aren't filthy, fierce animals. They're pets that were once loved. Still are." He glanced at Dandy, who was still bobbing around in the butterfly net. He aimed his ghost zapper at Bud.

Bud laughed. "Seriously? You think you can zap me?"

"Yep!" Malcolm fired, sending purple foam flying. But Bud blocked it with the net.

"Ew!" Dandy said, now plastered with kitty litter–sprinkled goo. But just as quickly, Dandy's eyebrows rose and his mouth curved into a smirk. He grabbed handfuls of the foam and reached through the net, slinging it at the ghost.

"No!" Bud dropped the net and backed away.

Dandy untangled himself, escaped, and ran after Bud, hurling zapper foam. The guy was so busy dodging Dandy that his litter storm died. That gave Malcolm enough time to flip off the electric switch. Once the cages lost power, there was nothing holding back the ghostly critters. They were instantly out and on the move.

"Oh no!" Bud yelled. He turned and took off running.

Chapter 10

High-Speed Chase

The room erupted into barks and hisses as the animals raced out after Bud. Silvia the snake slithered at rocket speed, while hamsters and gerbils scampered behind.

"He's getting away!" Malcolm shouted. He and Dandy took off too, dashing after them. Dandy's foam-soaked sneakers squished with each step.

The parade of ghostly animals rushed after Bud as he bolted down the street. A few dogs got close, but the dogcatcher sped up,

kicking up his heels to keep his backside from being bitten.

"They're heading toward the mall!" Dandy huffed, pumping his arms wildly.

Bud cut through the parking lot, the herd still on his tail. Within seconds, he was inside Tandy's Toy Shop.

The boys got there in time to see Bud speeding down the main aisle, knocking over bouncy balls and action figures. Game pieces went flying in the pet stampede.

"Hey!" a store clerk called as Malcolm and Dandy danced around the mess and out into the mall. They couldn't stop now!

The ghostly bunch tore through the mall, weaving around shoppers who screamed and dropped their packages.

As they reached the center, Malcolm saw the fashion show stage. The music played

and the crowd oohed. Cocoa had just begun sauntering down the runway.

She'd barely made it halfway down when Bud jumped on the stage, hoping to get away from his vicious posse. But they streamed after him. He easily whisked past Cocoa. But the animals stormed by, making her twist and twirl and do what Cocoa does best, scream her lungs out. "Ahhhhhh!"

She wasn't the only one screaming. The audience shrieked and scattered in all directions.

Malcolm and Dandy pushed through the crowd and looked around. They'd lost sight of Bud. Then Malcolm spotted him. "There!"

He and Dandy shared a nervous glance.

The dogcatcher had just entered Flour Power, the mall's most haunted bakery!

Chapter 11

Flour Power Face-Off

As they reached the doors, a herd of bakery workers ran out, throwing off their aprons and screaming, "I quit!"

Malcolm and Dandy pushed past them, hurried inside, and stopped short. What a mess! Eggs sailed, butter splatted, and flour sifted through the air. Malcolm and Dandy ducked, dodging a Boston cream pie that whizzed over their heads.

Then Malcolm saw the real target for the pie. Bud stood on a table, surrounded by all

the animals, Spooky included. A bunch of bakery ghosts were there too, pelting him with everything from baking soda to candy sprinkles.

Bud danced about, yelling at them. "I'll lock you all up, you brutes!"

"No, you won't!" Malcolm yelled. He pulled the zapper's trigger, covering the dogcatcher from head to toe. Within seconds, he was a purple puddle on the table.

The animals went from vicious to victorious, wagging and purring and prancing with joy.

Yip! Yip! Spooky bounded toward Malcolm and Dandy.

Malcolm smiled. "You're safe now, boy."

"What about them?" Dandy asked, pointing to the human ghosts who'd been haunting the bakery.

Right then, a thin lady ghost cocked her head and said, "Fifi?" A Great Dane loped to her and jumped up, placing his hefty paws on her shoulders. "Oh, Fifi!" she cried. The dog smothered her in puppy kisses.

Another ghost called out, "Silvia!" The snake slithered up his arm.

Soon, all the bakery ghosts were petting and playing with the animal ghosts.

A small ghost with an oversized mustache tugged on Malcolm's shirt. "Are you going to zap us, too?"

Malcolm raised an eyebrow. "That depends. Are you still going to haunt the bakery?"

The man grinned. "Not if I can adopt this little fellow." He held out a wiggly gerbil.

Malcolm lowered the zapper. "He's all yours."

"Thanks!" the ghost said. "And we're sorry about the mess. It's just that we all miss eating dessert. It's so unfair watching everyone else enjoy it."

Dandy nodded. "That *would* be rough."

The boys watched the ghosts happily leave with their new and old pets by their sides.

On Sunday morning, Malcolm rubbed the sleep goo from his eyes and sat up in bed. His only plans were to have a big bowl of Choco-Flakes and spend the rest of the day playing with Spooky.

Just as he walked into the kitchen, the phone rang. Grandma Eunice snatched it up first. "Hello?"

Cocoa stood by, bouncing on her toes.

Grandma Eunice scribbled on a note pad. She repeatedly mumbled, "Uh-huh. Yes. Of course."

"Who is it? Who is it?" Cocoa nearly hopped out of her shoes.

"Okay, thanks," Grandma Eunice said before hanging up the phone. "We've got another one!"

Cocoa rocketed into the air. "Yes!"

Malcolm glanced from Cocoa to his great-grandma. "You've got another what?"

"Another modeling gig," Grandma Eunice said, clacking her dentures. "The phone's been ringing off the hook all morning."

"What?" Malcolm couldn't believe it. "You? Why?"

"Because of this," Cocoa said, shoving a newspaper toward him.

He looked down at a full-page photo labeled "Chaos on the Catwalk." The ghostly pets were frozen in action on the runway. Cocoa was mid-pose, with Silvia the snake twisted around her arms.

"See?" she said to Malcolm. "I'm famous!"

Malcolm smiled. *Good,* he thought. *At least she'll be out of the house more.*

Malcolm grabbed his bowl of cereal and headed out of the kitchen. "If anyone needs me, I'll be down in the basement."

Questions for You

From Ghost Detectors
Malcolm and Dandy

Malcolm: I was super worried when Dandy and I couldn't find Spooky. Do you have a family pet? Has it ever been lost? What happened?

Dandy: I was determined to track down Spooky. I love that dog! Have you ever felt determined to do something that you might normally be scared to do? What was it?

Malcolm: Sometimes I just don't understand Cocoa. Do you have a sibling that you don't have anything in common with? How do you get along?

Dandy: Malcolm and I visited our local animal shelter to look for Spooky. Have you ever been to an animal shelter? What kinds of animals did you see?

To my mom and dad, thank you for everything —AE
A special thanks to my Melissa —DS

abdopublishing.com

Published by Magic Wagon, a division of ABDO, PO Box 398166, Minneapolis, Minnesota 55439. Copyright © 2016 by Abdo Consulting Group, Inc. International copyrights reserved in all countries. No part of this book may be reproduced in any form without written permission from the publisher. Calico™ is a trademark and logo of Magic Wagon.

Printed in the United States of America, North Mankato, Minnesota.
042015
092015

Written by Adrienne Enderle
Illustrated by Dave Shephard
Edited by Rochelle Baltzer, Heidi M.D. Elston, Megan M. Gunderson & Bridget O'Brien
Designed by Jillian O'Brien

Library of Congress Control Number: 2015942389

Cataloging-in-Publication Data

Enderle, Adrienne.
 Doggone! / Adrienne Enderle ; illustrated by David Shephard.
  p. cm. -- (Ghost detectors ; book 20)
Summary: Malcolm and Dandy are about to hunt down a ghost at a local bakery whey they realize they have a bigger problem on their hands. Their ghost dog, Spooky, is missing! The boys grab their ghost-detecting gear and set out on a mission to find their precious pooch. Things get hairy as they visit a pet cemetery, and animal shelter, and come face-to-face with the dognapper who took Spooky! Can Malcolm and Dandy save Spooky, or will they be separated from their furry friend?
ISBN 978-1-62402-103-9
1. Ghost stories. 2. Dogs¬--Juvenile fiction. 3. Animal shelters--Juvenile fiction. 4. Animal rescue--Juvenile fiction. 5. Haunted places--Juvenile fiction.
6. Humorous stories. [1.Ghosts--Fiction. 2. Dogs--Fiction. 3. Animal shelters--Fiction. 4. Animal rescue--Fiction. 5. Haunted places--Fiction. 6. Humorous stories.]   I. Shephard, Dave, illustrator. II. Title.
813.6--dc23
[Fic]
                                                              2015942389